Overtime
Polar Bears vs Thunde

MW00966155

Hello sports fans, this hockey game is tied at 2 goals each and we are going into Overtime. The fans are on the edge of their seats. Will the Thunderbirds or the Polar Bears score the next goal to win the game? Wow, we are in for an exciting finish as the players are ready and Overtime is about to begin. Let's check out the action!

ISBN 978-0-9808866-3-4

Practice early reading skills using the special page format.
- see our Literacy Guide on page 54 -

Support the literacy development of all children.
www.boysRreading.com

ColorSports Publishing Inc.

ColourSports Publishing Inc. - 5 Livingstone Dr. - Dundas - L9H 7S3 - Ontario - Canada

Printed in China

Hello sports fans, boys and girls, parents, grammas and gramps.
Who will win this big hockey game and be this year's new champs?

Will the Polar Bears win, they are so big and can really skate.
The blue, grey and white check hard with all their body weight.

Or will the Thunderbirds win by using their great skating agility?
The red, white and black attack fast with quick scoring ability.

After 3 periods the score is tied at 2, so the game has not ended.
The teams will now play an extra period, so the game is extended.

A a
B b
C c
D d
E e
F f
G g
H h
I i
J j
K k
L l
M m
N n
O o
P p
Q q
R r
S s
T t
U u
V v
W w
X x
Y y
Z z

SAVE THE TREES

THE FINAL MINUTES
03:00 → 02:00 → 01:00 → 00:00

World Peace GREAT TEAM PLAY

CHAMPIONSHIP DAY

All eyes are on center-ice, as the players catch their breath.

All eyes on center-ice players catch breath Everyone ready for overtime it's called sudden death

Everyone is ready for overtime,
and it's called sudden death.

A a

B b

C c

D d

E e

F f

G g

H h

I i

J j

K k

L l

M m

N n

O o

P p

Q q

R r

S s

T t

U u

V v

W w

X x

Y y

Z z

The players wait at center-ice for the puck drop by the referee.

players wait center-ice puck drop by referee Set face-off team that scores next earns victory

xciting Play-By-Play Action

Set for the face-off, the team that scores next earns the victory.

A Thunderbird takes the puck to the blueline and shoots it in quick.

Thunderbird takes puck blueline shoots in quick Bear defenseman tries check him flies off stick

As a Bear defenseman tries to check him, the puck flies off his stick.

The Birds skate in for the puck led
by one of their strong forwards.

Birds
skate
puck
led
one
their
strong
forwards
But
Bear
gets
first
shoots
along
boards

But a Bear gets to it first and
shoots it up along the boards.

A a
B b
C c
D d
E e
F f
G g
H h
I i
J j
K k
L l
M m
N n
O o
P p
Q q
R r
S s
T t
U u
V v
W w
X x
Y y
Z z

©C.HICKS/96

The Thunderbird checks the
Polar Bear and breaks up the play

Thunderbird checks Polar Bear breaks up play turns skates towards net after stealing the puck away

He turns and skates towards the net after stealing the puck away.

A a
B b
C c
D d
E e
F f
G g
H h
I i
J j
K k
L l
M m
N n
O o
P p
Q q
R r
S s
T t
U u
V v
W w
X x
Y y
Z z

©C.HICKS/96

He fires the puck at the goal, while a forward tries to deflect it.

fires
puck
goal
while
forward
tries
deflect
Bear
goalie
stops
sliding
across
net
protect
it

The Bear goalie stops the puck,
sliding across his net to protect it.

A a

B b

C c

D d

E e

F f

G g

H h

I i

J j

K k

L l

M m

N n

O o

P p

Q q

R r

S s

T t

U u

V v

W w

X x

Y y

Z z

Wow! What a save! The goalie grabs the puck to cover the rebound.

Wow

What

save

goalie

grabs

puck

cover

rebound

Oh

chance

Birds

look

hover

all

around

Oh! What a chance! The Birds look for the puck and hover all around.

At the face-off the goalie sets up in his stance to cut down the angle

face-off

goalie

sets

stance

cut

down

angle

sticks

slash

down

puck

slides

free

centermen

tangle

The sticks slash down and the puck slides free as the centermen tangle.

A a
B b
C c
D d
E e
F f
G g
H h
I i
J j
K k
L l
M m
N n
O o
P p
Q q
R r
S s
T t
U u
V v
W w
X x
Y y
Z z

A Bear forward skates out quickly and breaks away with the puck.

Bear

forward

skates

quickly

breaks

away

puck

Bird

defenseman

falls

turns

skate

blade

gets

stuck

A Bird defenseman falls as he turns
and his skate blade gets stuck.

A a
B b
C c
D d
E e
F f
G g
H h
I i
J j
K k
L l
M m
N n
O o
P p
Q q
R r
S s
T t
U u
V v
W w
X x
Y y
Z z

Two Bears skate fast as they pass the puck, it's a two-on-one break.

Two

Bears

skate

fast

pass

puck

two-on-one

break

defenseman

skates

back

Bear

gives

him

fake

A defenseman skates back as the Bear with the puck gives him a fake.

A a
B b
C c
D d
E e
F f
G g
H h
I i
J j
K k
L l
M m
N n
O o
P p
Q q
R r
S s
T t
U u
V v
W w
X x
Y y
Z z

He stick-handles the puck down the right side into the Birds' zone.

03:00 → 02:00 → 01:00 → 00:00

stick-handles

puck

down

right

side

into

Birds'

zone

turns

passes

out

front

Bear

all

alone

©C.HICKS/96

Then he turns and passes the puck out front to a Bear all alone.

A a
B b
C c
D d
E e
F f
G g
H h
I i
J j
K k
L l
M m
N n
O o
P p
Q q
R r
S s
T t
U u
V v
W w
X x
Y y
Z z

Whack! It's a slap-shot, the goalie
flies across in a frantic flop.

Whack slap-shot goalie flies across frantic flop Thud puck hits pad slides making gigantic stop

Thud! The puck hits his pad, as he slides making a gigantic stop.

A a
B b
C c
D d
E e
F f
G g
H h
I i
J j
K k
L l
M m
N n
O o
P p
Q q
R r
S s
T t
U u
V v
W w
X x
Y y
Z z

The Bear winger is on the rebound
and shoots a backhand shot quick.

Bear

winger

rebound

shoots

backhand

shot

quick

Bird

goalie

stops

puck

again

stick

pad

kick

Whoa! The Bird goalie stops the puck again with a stick and pad kick.

A a
B b
C c
D d
E e
F f
G g
H h
I i
J j
K k
L l
M m
N n
O o
P p
Q q
R r
S s
T t
U u
V v
W w
X x
Y y
Z z

©C.HICKS/96

Another hard shot is fired, but the Bird goalie sees the puck clearly.

Another hard shot fired goalie sees puck clearly cooly snags big trapper squeezes puck dearly

He cooly snags it with his big trapper then squeezes the puck dearly.

Wow! Three hard shots on the net bu
the goalie made save after save.

Wow

Three

hard

shots

net

goalie

made

after

save

waits

face-off

gets

rest

effort

gave

He waits for the face-off and gets a rest for the effort he gave.

A	a
B	b
C	c
D	d
E	e
F	f
G	g
H	h
I	i
J	j
K	k
L	l
M	m
N	n
O	o
P	p
Q	q
R	r
S	s
T	t
U	u
V	v
W	w
X	x
Y	y
Z	z

A Bird gets the puck, then looks for a way to skate it out and escape.

Bird

gets

puck

looks

skate

out

escape

sees

forward

stops

shoot

pass

right

on

tape

He sees a forward and stops to shoot him a pass, right on the tape.

A a
B b
C c
D d
E e
F f
G g
H h
I i
J j
K k
L l
M m
N n
O o
P p
Q q
R r
S s
T t
U u
V v
W w
X x
Y y
Z z

The fast skating Bird takes the puck
with a Bear in hot pursuit of him.

fast

skating

Bird

takes

puck

Bear

hot

pursuit

digs

hard

red-line

center

can

shoot

in

He digs in hard to the red-line
at center so he can shoot it in.

A a
B b
C c
D d
E e
F f
G g
H h
I i
J j
K k
L l
M m
N n
O o
P p
Q q
R r
S s
T t
U u
V v
W w
X x
Y y
Z z

The Bear goalie skates out of his net
to play the puck, he's out of position

Bear

goalie

skates

net

play

puck

out

position

net's

empty

gets

shoots

it

risky

decision

The net's empty as he gets the puck and shoots it out, a risky decision!

A B C D E F G H I J K L M N O P Q R S T U V W X Y Z
a b c d e f g h i j k l m n o p q r s t u v w x y z

A Bear reaches for the puck as he digs his skate blades in hard.

Bear

reaches

puck

digs

skate

blades

hard

Birds

change

fly

quick

pass

catches

them

off-guard

The Birds change on the fly but a quick pass catches them off-guard.

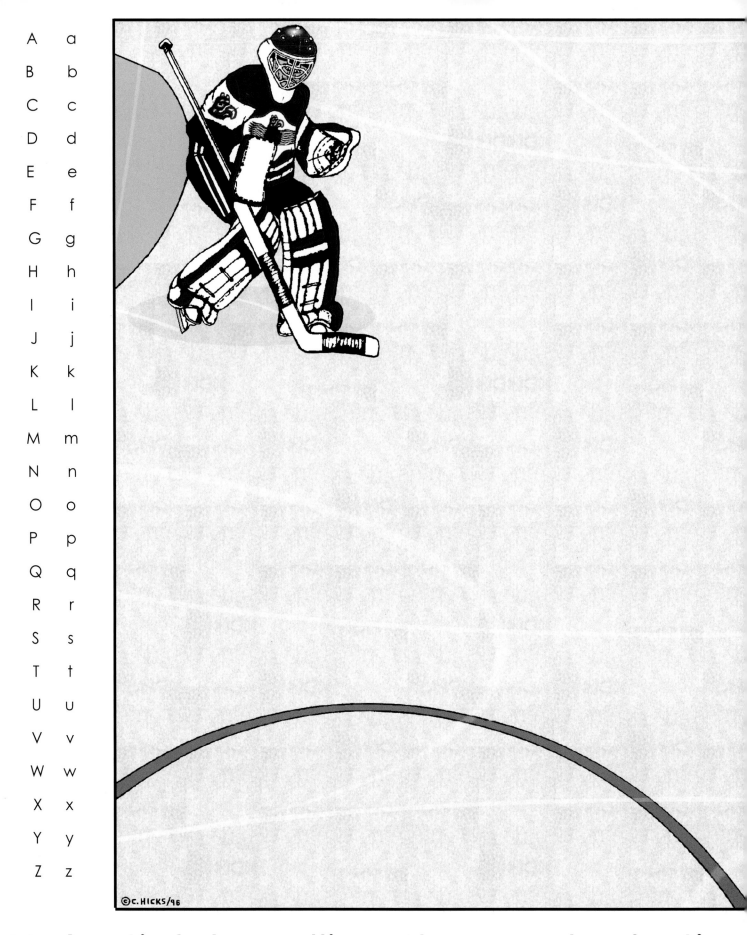

A a
B b
C c
D d
E e
F f
G g
H h
I i
J j
K k
L l
M m
N n
O o
P p
Q q
R r
S s
T t
U u
V v
W w
X x
Y y
Z z

©C.HICKS/96

He's stick-handling the puck, skating fast towards the Bird goaltender.

He's
stick-handling
puck
skating
fast
towards
Bird
goaltender
almost
break-away
racing
get
past
Bird
defender

He's almost on a break-away, racing
to get past the Bird defender.

Whack! The Polar Bear slaps the puck hard with a quick release.

Whack

Bear

slaps

puck

hard

quick

release

Thud

puck

hits

goalie's

pad

moves

out

crease

Thud! The puck hits the goalie's pad
as he moves out of his crease.

A a
B b
C c
D d
E e
F f
G g
H h
I i
J j
K k
L l
M m
N n
O o
P p
Q q
R r
S s
T t
U u
V v
W w
X x
Y y
Z z

The goalie falls back, kicking out his leg pad for the puck, as he twists.

goalie

falls

back

kicking

pad

twists

shoots

scores

Bear

slaps

puck

into

net

flicking

wrists

He shoots! He scores! A Bear slaps the puck into the net, flicking his wrists.

A   a
B   b
C   c
D   d
E   e
F   f
G   g
H   h
I   i
J   j
K   k
L   l
M   m
N   n
O   o
P   p
Q   q
R   r
S   s
T   t
U   u
V   v
W   w
X   x
Y   y
Z   z

The Polar Bears win! They jump for joy, as the fans cheer their good luck.

Polar

Bears

win

jump

joy

fans

cheer

good

luck

Thunderbirds

silent

sad

net

lies

puck

The Thunderbirds are silent and sad, for in their net lies the puck.

Wow! What great fun and excitement for the fans who came.
The Polar Bears and the Thunder Birds played an awesome game.

The players fought hard with no energy to spare.
In the heat of the battle they always played fair.

The players now walk about and greet one another.
They reach to shake hands showing respect for each other.

Yes, winning the championship is a sensation.
And, playing with sportsmanship wins admiration.

Hockey Player Positions

Forwards:

The three players who make up the attacking line or forward line of a team, the centerman, the right winger and the left winger. These three forwards will work together controlling and passing the puck to each other. They will try to get into a position to shoot the puck on the net to try and score a goal. They are usually fast skaters, skillful stick-handlers and can shoot the puck with speed and accuracy.

Centerman:

The center player in the forward line who skates up and down the ice in the middle area. He leads his team's attack when they are trying to score a goal and will take most of the face-offs. He is usually one of the strongest skaters and stick-handlers as he controls the puck a lot during offensive plays.

Left Winger:

The left-winger in the forward line skates up and down the left side of the ice. He controls the left side of the rink during his team's attack when they are trying to score a goal.

Right Winger:

The right-winger in the forward line skates up and down the right side of the ice. He controls the right side of the rink during his team's attack when they are trying to score a goal.

Defense:

The two players who play back during the action of a hockey game to defend their zone. They try to prevent any scoring chances by checking and covering the opposition players. While they mainly work to help the goalie prevent any goals from being scored they also will join the forwards at times to try and score goals.

Left Defenseman:

The player who plays on the left side of a team's defensive unit. The left defenseman covers the left half of the rink by checking any opponents with the puck trying to score a goal from this area.

Right Defenseman:

The player who plays on the right side of a team's defensive unit. The right defenseman covers the right half of the rink by checking any opponents with the puck trying to score a goal from this area.

Goaltender:

The player who guards the net to prevent the opponents from scoring a goal by stopping the puck. He will use his body, leg pads, arms, stick and gloves to stop the puck from going into his net. (He wears large protective equipment on his body as well as a face mask)

A a
B b
C c
D d
E e
F f
G g
H h
I i
J j
K k
L l
M m
N n
O o
P p
Q q
R r
S s
T t
U u
V v
W w
X x
Y y
Z z

Thunder Bird bench

THE FINAL MINUTES
03:00 → 02:00 → 01:00 → 00:00

SAVE THE TREES   World Peace   GREAT TEAM PLAY   CHAMPIONSHIP DAY

boards

left-winger

center-

left-defenseman

net

blue-line

goaltender

centerman

right-defenseman

right-winger

penalty boxes

Here are the Thunderbird forwards,
defencemen and goalie getting set

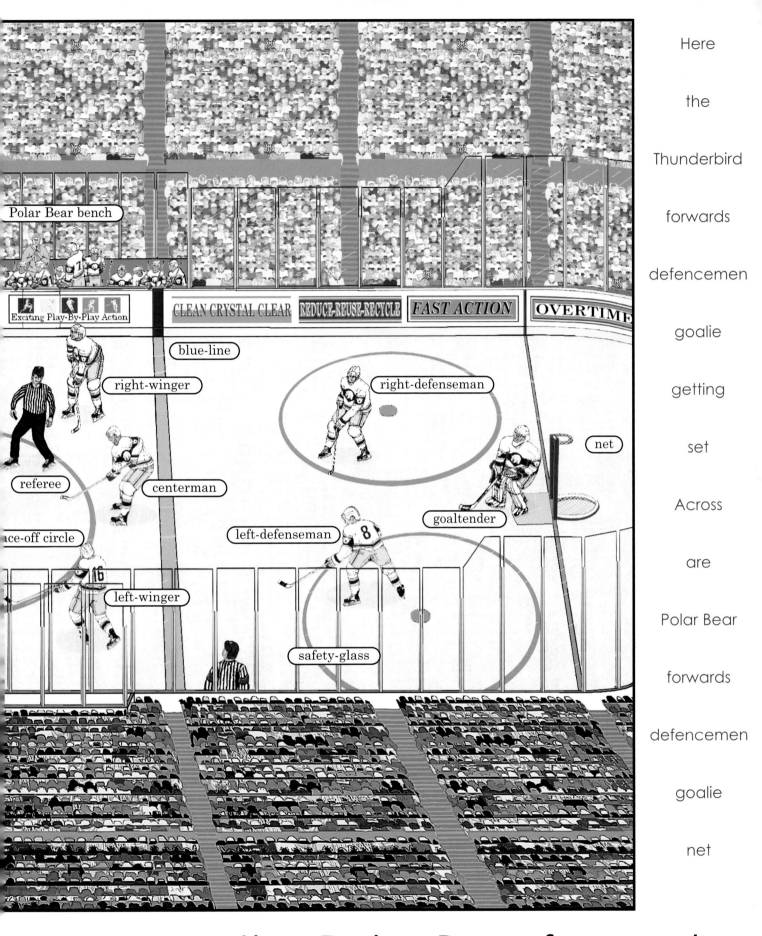

Polar Bear bench

Exciting Play-By-Play Action

CLEAN CRYSTAL CLEAR   REDUCE-REUSE-RECYCLE   FAST ACTION   OVERTIME

blue-line

right-winger

right-defenseman

referee

centerman

net

goaltender

left-defenseman

face-off circle

left-winger

safety-glass

Here

the

Thunderbird

forwards

defencemen

goalie

getting

set

Across

are

Polar Bear

forwards

defencemen

goalie

net

Across are the Polar Bear forwards, defencemen and their goalie in net.

51

Hockey Glossary

Assist: A player earns an assist when they pass the puck to another player who then scores a goal. (a maximum of two assists are credited for one goal)

Backcheck: When a player skates back towards his own zone to regain control of the puck by checking an opponent who has the puck.

Backhand shot: A shot made from a player who is not facing the net, his back is towards the net. (a forehand shot is taken by a player when he is facing his target, the net)

Blue lines: The two blue lines running across the ice that are used in determining off-sides. (The puck must cross the blueline before an attacking player or it will be called an off-side.)

Boards: The wooden or fiberglass short wall that surrounds the ice rink to keep the puck on the ice surface during the game.

Body check: When a player tries to stop his opponent by bumping or slaming into him with either his hip or shoulder. This is only allowed against an opponent in control of the puck.

Break-away: When a player with the puck skates in alone on the goalie to try and score agoal.

Center face-off circle: A large circle at the center of the ice where the puck is dropped during a face-off to start the game and to restart the game after a goal has been scored.

Center ice: The area between the two blue-lines, also called the neutral zone.

Change on-the-fly: When either team changes their players on the ice while the game action is underway They must do it very quickly not to give the other team an advantage.

Check or checking: When a player tries to stop or slow down an opponent. A player can check with his stick or body to try and get the puck away from an opponent.

Crease: The semi-circular area marked on the ice in front of the net is the goalie's crease. Players are not allowed to stand in this area, it is the goalie's area.

Cut down the angle: When the goalie gets his position ready to stop the puck from going into his net. He will move toward where the puck is, to block more of his net and make a save.

Deflect: When a player causes the puck to change direction, by touching it with the blade of the hockey stick. A shot on the net can be deflected to fool the goalie and score a goal.

Face-off: When the puck is dropped by the referee between two opposing players facing each other. The players have their stick blades flat on the ice and try to control the puck for their team. A face-off begins the hockey action of each period or starts the play again after it has stopped.

Flop: When a goalie goes down on his knees to stop the puck with his legs pads.

Goal: A goal is scored when the puck goes between the goalposts into the net. It can glide along the ice or fly through the air but it must cross the red line between the goalposts to be a goal.

Goalie or goaltender: (goalkeeper) The player who guards the net to prevent the opponents from scoring a goal by stopping the puck any way he can. (He wears large protective equipment and a face mask)

cing: When a player with the puck shoots it from behind the red-line at center-ice across the oppnent's goal line. (a face-off comes all the way back to that player's team zone)

let: The netting attached to the frame of the goal to trap the puck when a goal is scored.

Off-side When an attacking player skates across the opponent's blue line before the puck is passed or carried into the zone. The puck must go across the blue-line first before an attacking player can.

Overtime: An extra period of play used when the game is tied after three periods have been played.

enalty: When a player breaks a rule he will recieve a penalty from the referee. He usually will serve 2 minutes in the penalty box and his team will play short one player for that time period. (some 2 minute penalties can be given for holding, tripping, hooking, interference, high-sticking and slashing while 5 minute penalties can be given for fighting and hitting (body-checking) from behind or boarding)

eriod: 20-minutes of playing time, there are three periods in a hockey game.

uck: The black, hard rubber disc, used to play hockey. It glides on the ice or flies through the air.

ebound: A puck that bounces off the goalie's body, pads, goalie stick or equipment.

eferees: The officials in a hockey game. They watch all the action closely to make sure all the rules are followed so the game is played fairly. They watch for and call any penalties and make decisions about goals scored.

elease: The act of shooting the puck. When a player flexes his hands and arms to propel his stick against the puck to make a shot. (a wrist shot, slap shot, snap shot or backhand shot)

ight on the tape: When a player passes the puck and aims for the tape on his teamate's stick blade.

ave: When a goalie blocks or stops the puck to prevent a goal.

cores: When a player shoots the puck into the net of the opposing team for a goal.

lap shot: When a player swings his stick high in a backswing and then swings fast and hard down on the puck. The puck flies off the stick at a high rate of speed.

tick and pad kick: When a goalie makes a save by kicking out the puck with his stick and leg pad at the same time.

tick-handling: When a player controls the puck with the blade of his stick by gliding the puck back and forth, and/or forward and back while skating.

udden-death overtime: An overtime period that ends as soon as one team scores a goal. The team that scores first in sudden-death overtime wins the game.

rapper: A big glove a goalie wears on one hand used to catch the puck when making a save.

wo-on-one break: When two attacking players skate with the puck against one defensive player.

Vrist shot: A shot made using a strong flicking of the wrist and forearm muscles, with the stick blade kept on the ice. It is not as fast as a slap shot but it is more accurate.

amboni: The machine used to clean the ice in between the periods. (it scraps off the snow and spreads a thin layer of water that freezes quickly)

Literacy Guide

Practice early reading skills using the special page format.

The special page format is designed to enhance the opportunity for children to practice key skills in their reading development. The chart below highlights 4 specific skills that are fundamental building blocks required to produce a new reader. Along with the story text in black at the bottom of each story scene there are letters in blue on the left and words in red on the right as a quick and handy reference to practice some of these skills.

Use their current ability as a guide to focus on the appropriate skills to practice.

4 Building Blocks Of Reading - With Suggested Reading Skills Activities

Oral Language Development

Speaking aloud and expressing ideas and thoughts builds oral language skills and provides an essential foundation for the development of reading.

Suggested Activities

- look through the story letting the child talk and tell about the pictures using their own words

- encourage, listen and actively respond to the child's own words, thoughts and ideas

- prompt for more oral discussion and detail with questions and rephrasing their words and ideas

- take turns talking about the action and what the players and fans might be feeling, thinking and saying

Letter and Sound Recognition

An essential pre-reading skill is recognizing all the letters (upper and lower case) of the alphabet and the sounds that they make.

Suggested Activities

- together point to each blue letter, name and make the sound of each letter in the alphabet

- explain letters have a lower case (small) symbol and upper case (big) symbol

- name a letter, the sound it makes and then have your child point to it (take turns making it a fun game)

- identify a letter and see if it can be found in a red word on the left and in the story (letters make words)

Building Word Vocabulary

An important reading skill development is the ability to visually identify words, to recognize the grouping of letters and to remember the word meaning.

Suggested Activities

- point to and say a red word, name each letter and their sounds that group together making each word

- point to and read a red word and then let your child find it in the story sentence (take turns making it a game)

- take turns pointing to and reading aloud each red word from the top to bottom in order

- point to a red word, have your child say the word and explain it's meaning (make a sentence with the word)

Reading Fluency and Comprehension

Developing the ability to read words accurately and understand their meaning at the same time produces a fluent and competent reader.

Suggested Activities

- read the story together, develop a rythym and use the rhyme to create and model a natural reading fluency

- ask questions about the action and events to check for memory and understanding

- discuss the thinking, emotions and feelings of the many players and spectators watching the game

- talk about team work, fair-play and sportsmanship, allowing your child to express their feelings and ideas

Find a good balance between working with your child's current abilities and challenging them to learn!

Please support the literacy development of your child.